Nicky

Davy

Donny

Daisy

Copyright © 2000 by Nord-Süd Verlag AG, Gossau Zürich, Switzerland
First published in Switzerland under the title *Herzlichen Glückwunsch, Pauli*
English translation copyright © 2000 by North-South Books Inc.
First published in the United States, Great Britain, Canada,
Australia, and New Zealand in 2000 by North-South Books,
an imprint of Nord-Süd Verlag AG, Gossau Zürich, Switzerland.
Distributed in the United States by North-South Books Inc., New York.

Library of Congress Cataloging-in-Publication Data is available.
A CIP catalogue record for this book is available from The British Library.
ISBN 0-7358-1345-0 (trade binding) 10 9 8 7 6 5 4 3 2 1
ISBN 0-7358-1346-9 (library binding) 10 9 8 7 6 5 4 3 2 1
Printed in Belgium

For more information about our books, and the authors and artists
who create them, visit our web site: www.northsouth.com

Other books in the Davy series

What Have You Done, Davy?
Where Have You Gone, Davy?
Will You Mind the Baby, Davy?
What's the Matter, Davy?
Merry Christmas, Davy!
Why Are You Fighting, Davy?

Happy Birthday,
Davy!

Brigitte Weninger
Illustrated by Eve Tharlet
Translated by Rosemary Lanning

A MICHAEL NEUGEBAUER BOOK
NORTH-SOUTH BOOKS / NEW YORK / LONDON

"How much longer is it
 till my birthday?"
 asked Davy.
"You've asked me that a
 hundred times," said
 Mother Rabbit, hiding
 a smile.
"I know," said Davy.
"But how much longer?"
"It's ten more days,"
 said Mother.
"That long?" cried Davy.

But soon it was seven more days, then five, then three. . . .
Davy was so excited, he couldn't sit still.
Father Rabbit was telling them a story about a little rabbit
who had three wishes: ". . . so all his wishes came true, and
he hopped happily back to his burrow."
"I love that story," said Daisy. "Tell it again, please!"
"No. I'm sorry. I have work to do," said Father Rabbit.
"Oh!" said Davy, with a disappointed sigh. "If *I* had a wish I
would ask for someone who always had time to tell stories."

The next morning it rained so hard that the
rabbit children had to stay indoors. By the
afternoon they had run out of things to do.
"Let's play tag," suggested Donny.
"We've played that already," said Dan.
"Want play ball!" squeaked little Dinah.
But they soon got bored with that, too.
Davy stared gloomily out at the rain.
"If *I* had a wish," he muttered, "I would
ask for someone to teach us more games."

The following morning, Davy couldn't find anyone with time to play. They were all too busy getting ready for his birthday. Davy was pleased about that, but he was bored on his own.

"You know, Nicky," he said to his toy rabbit, "if *I* had a wish, I would ask for someone who had lots of time to spend with me."

At last it was Davy's birthday!

He woke to hear the whole family singing, "Happy Birthday, dear Davy!"

Dan had made him a beautiful garland. "When you wear this, everyone will know it's your birthday," he said.

"Thank you!" said Davy. "It's great!"

He had to wait until his party that afternoon for the rest of his presents. Waiting was very hard!

Finally it was time for
the party, but where were
the presents?
"Davy dear, Mother and I
listened to all your wishes," said
Father, smiling, "but the present
we chose was much too big to
wrap. So we hid it somewhere
in the burrow. See if you can
find it!"

Davy's heart began to pound. Could his present really be that big? What could it be? He looked around the room, but he couldn't see anything. There was no present in his bedroom. Was it under Mother Rabbit's bed? No! But there was something behind the larder door. . . .

"Grandpa! Granny!" Davy gave them both a hug.
"Many happy returns of the day, Davy dear,"
said his grandparents, laughing.
"We are your birthday present this year, and
we have brought a whole sackful of time with
us. Time for stories, time for games, and
time for anything else you want to do."

There were still more presents for Davy: a shiny pebble from Eddie, a toy tea set from Daisy and Donny, which they had made themselves, and a kiss and hug from Dinah. Grandpa and Granny gave him a big book of stories.

"Now we can read you a new story every day," said Mother.

"But what will we do when we have read them all?" asked Davy anxiously.

"We'll go back to the beginning again!" said Father. "A good story is worth repeating."

"Now we'll teach you the games we played when we were young," said Grandpa. They showed the children how to play "Simon Says" and statues and musical chairs. And they played and played until Mother called them for supper. Then they played some more. Davy didn't win many games, but he didn't mind at all. He was happy.

After supper, the birthday boy was allowed to choose a story. He held the new storybook while Grandpa read aloud, and everyone listened, enthralled. Then Granny told the children about all the pranks she and Grandpa used to play when they were young. Davy liked those stories best of all.

By now the children were
very tired. It had been a
long, exciting day.

Only Davy was still awake. "That was my best birthday ever," he whispered to his grandparents. "And when it's your birthday, you can wish for a little rabbit to play with you and love you. Then I will come and be *your* birthday present."

"What a good idea," said Granny,
    as Davy snuggled in Grandpa's arms
    and fell fast asleep.